Sister Bishop's Christmas Miracle

Sister Bishop's Christmas Miracle

Janene Wolsey Baadsgaard

Bookcraft
Salt Lake City, Utah

All characters in this book are fictitious,
and any resemblance to actual persons,
living or dead, is purely coincidental.

Library of Congress Catalog Card Number 98-74224
ISBN 1-57008-573-0

First Printing, 1998

Printed in the United States of America

Chapter One

My bishop regularly informs me I make *much* too big a deal out of everything and I ought to knock it off because it always gets us both in a lot of hot water. I know he's right but sometimes I can't help myself. He ought to know; I've been married to the man for over twenty years.

Whenever I start getting big ideas, my husband, Vern, reminds me about last year's ward Christmas program . . . then he gives me the don't-you-even-think-about-it look. Of course we both know that even I, LaRue Mess-up Willey, can't top last year.

Close as I can figure, this whole Christmas program business started about the time I finally got Willey child number eight off to kindergarten. I allowed this knock-on-wood thought to whiz through my brain, *Hey, maybe I could lose twenty pounds.*

Next thing I know Vern says, "LaRue, the stake president called. Said he wants to talk to both of us down at his office on Thursday night."

"That means it's something big," I answered with a gulp. "They never ask both the husband and wife to come down together unless it's something big. We can always say no. Nobody'd ever know but us and the stake president."

"Someone else would know," Vern answered, looking up.

Boy, it sure bugs me whenever Vern's right and I'm wrong and he feels the need to let me know. Now, as any self-respecting Mormon knows, there's nothing quite as tremulous as hearing from your stake president. It's bad enough when you're asked to go *alone* to the stake offices on a dark and stormy Thursday night, but when the stake president asks to see you and your husband *together,* you pretty much better count on changing your life forever right then and there.

"Father in Heaven," I prayed after the stake President called Vern to be bishop, "remember me? LaRue here. I'm the one who's gonna lose twenty pounds. Hadn't planned on being the bishop's wife. I don't know heads or tails about how to be a bishop's wife."

Well, next thing I know I'm sobbing during

milk commercials on television . . . a real emotional basket case, if you know what I mean. Vern just rolled his eyes; he's used to me doing weird things for absolutely no reason.

I figured at my age, forty-three and a half, it must be the change of life or something. Logical, right? Kept waiting for those hot flashes, alias power surges, I'd heard about during Relief Society homemaking meetings for years. Figured I should've paid more attention to those change-of-life lectures instead of the cooking demonstrations. But heck, they give out samples you can eat at the cooking demonstrations. Always thought it was dumb to call it menopause anyhow, when men don't do any pausing at all. At least it should be called womenopause or something more fitting.

Next thing I know I'm sporting a two-piece paper hankie at the obstetrician's office and Doc Dillard flat out told me then and there.

"I'm going through the change, right?" I quizzed after the examination. "Just a little change of life, right? Nothing to worry about, *right?*"

"You're going through a change, all right, LaRue, just not the change you figured on," Doc Dillard answered.

Right away I determined being pregnant when you're definitely over the hill is a lot like being the new bishop's wife. First you're sorta in shock, numb-like—and everybody congratulates you. Then right soon the honeymoon's over and you realize you're in way over your head. Most of the time I feel like Bambi in the headlights, wondering, *What have I got myself into?*

It's not exactly easy being unselfish, you know. It's real hard work—especially giving up your body and the rest of your life so you can create nine brand-new babies and take good care of them, or giving up your time and your husband to help the less fortunate when you figure you could sure use your time and your husband's help about as much as anybody else. Me and Vern's been puzzling over how to take good care of our family *and* five hundred ward members without neglecting anybody. Mostly we feel downright inadequate. So we have to pray a lot, and I mean a lot. The way I got it figured, children are the only real important thing in life—everything else is fluff—and we're all God's children.

Being a pregnant bishop's wife sure gives a body lots of chances to practice being charitable, even though you'd rather take a nap. Most Mormons are pretty good about trying not to monopolize too much of their bishop's time. But some members assume their bishop, who is just a regular guy like Vern, with a full-time job and a family to raise like everybody else, should be on call twenty-*five* hours a day, *eight* days a week—a sort of jack-of-all-trades religious doctor with unlimited office hours, no partners, and *no* vacation time. They go to him for *everything.* So bishops tend to become the invisible man to their own families.

When Vern dashes home between work, meetings, hospital visits, or ward activities to grab a cold fritter, and my children ask, "Who's that stranger, Mommy?" I answer, "Can't say if I know. Looks familiar, but can't quite place him."

Since the bishop sits up on the stand behind the pulpit during sacrament meeting and tries to keep a lid on the ward kettle during Sunday School, priesthood, Relief Society, and Primary meetings, I always sit alone with our children while we're at church.

Had one woman sitting in the pew behind me say once, "That's a lot of work for you, dragging all those kids to church every Sunday while your husband's off hunting and fishing."

Never bothered to correct her. Guess I just don't look like a bishop's wife. Not sure how to act like one either. When our former bishop was in, everybody knew it was really his wife, Beatrice, who ran the show. Like when Bishop Beebe made an announcement from the pulpit about the upcoming ward party, saying, "We'll be having our annual hamburger fry down at North Park this Wednesday at seven," everybody would turn and look at Beatrice to see if he got it right.

"That's six-thirty, Herman," Beatrice Beebe would bellow right from her pew. "And tell 'em to bring their own dishes and lawn chairs if they don't want to get their personalities wet."

Beatrice didn't raise her hand or any-thing, just hollered right out loud and no-body thought two cents about it; pretty much the way things were, that's all. Let's just say Beatrice, built like an offensive line-man, knew how to get things done. Me, I'm built more like the school mascot, goofing off on the sidelines. People usually laugh at me and figure I don't know what's going on because frankly I usually don't.

Now, Beatrice, she was a terrific bishop's wife. Sure knew how to make people jump. Take for instance her food assignments for all the ward socials. If you didn't sign up on the clipboard paper passed around during Relief Society volunteer-like, Beatrice'd call you up and *tell* you what to bring. If Beatrice says you have to bring potato salad and baked beans to the ward hamburger fry, you better bring potato salad and baked beans. If you bring potato salad and baked beans, you might as well show up and eat too. We always had real good turnouts to the ward parties when Beatrice ran things.

Me, when I tell people to do something, they mostly stare back at me like the light's on but nobody's home. People, as a general rule, don't even notice me until I do something dumb, which, come to think of it, is quite often. I've had this problem for a long time. Like for instance when I was in high school, I got a huge megaphone stuck in my mouth and I wasn't even a cheerleader.

I was goofing off on the sidelines at a basketball game trying to get the crowd to chant, "Ooga, Ooga, Booga Babe. Spanish Fork is here to stay. Scuttle, muttle, vooda bum. Spanish Fork just can't be won."

Nobody listened. Nobody cheered. Nobody even noticed me till I tried to pull that huge horn out of my mouth. Problem was my double-jointed jaw got stuck. Before I knew it, the whole student body was rolling in the bleachers watching me tug. I tried sauntering off the sidelines real nonchalantly-like. Didn't work. See, I don't try to be stupid, but things tend to turn out weird for me.

Everyone knows I'm not running things in the ward, because my husband hardly ever talks to me. He's one of those nonverbal males, you know, the kind who only use words to avoid saying anything. Being pregnant didn't help. Ward members figure the bishop's much too busy for things like that. They suppose I must have got myself in this predicament all by my lonesome and I'm old enough to know better.

Months after Bishop Beebe was released and Vern was put in, I heard someone say, "You mean that clueless lady with the really weird laugh who looks like she swallowed a basketball is the bishop's wife?"

It's embarrassing. It's not like I *try* to snort when I laugh, *try* to look like I just swallowed a basketball, or *try* to be totally clueless. But I figure I'll just have to make the best of things the way they are. The way I see it, life can still be better than bearable even if I do snort and get pregnant when I'm old enough to be somebody's grandma. And there are definitely some advantages to being clueless. You don't get any credit but you don't have to take any blame either.

I've never even come close to filling Beatrice's shoes. I'd feel downright odd hollering out in church because, frankly, I never know what to holler about. My husband only moves his lips when it's necessary to relay important information like, "Please pass the potato salad and baked beans."

Guess he figures I have 'bout all the information I can handle. Me, I talk all the time. Almost never stop. That's probably why we wound up married. Works out real well while you're courting and for the first few days of marital bliss, then you start driving each other crazy.

Now, as if all this pregnant bishop's wife stuff wasn't enough, next thing I know I'm being called out of Sunday School class for an interview by one of my husband's counselors in the bishopric.

"Sister Willey," Brother Reese smiled as he ushered me into my husband's office. "Come right on in here and take a seat. How are you doing, Sister Willey? Well, don't you look just fine. My, haven't we blossomed."

I'm sitting there thinking, *Blossomed slossomed. I guess that's better than saying, "My, haven't we gotten fat." Get to the point, man. This must be pretty bad or he wouldn't have to butter me up like this.*

Brother Reese squirmed in his chair and cleared his throat. "Sister Willey, we'd sure like you to be in charge of the ward Christmas program this year."

I'm thinking, *If being the bishop's wife, complete with number nine in the oven, doesn't get you out of surprises like this or at least give you fair warning they're coming, what good is being bishop's wife? Is Vern crazy?*

"Have you run this past my husband?" I asked, eyebrows lowered to half-mast.

"Oh, yes. Bishop says you love creative challenges like this," Brother Reese smiled through his gaping teeth. His bow tie was so tight it made his bald head look like it was ready to explode. "So what do you say, Sister Willey? Will you help us out this year?"

What I wanted to say was, *"What! Are you crazy! Can't you tell I'm about to explode? Are you daft?"*

What I actually said was, "Sure, Brother Reese, I'd love to."

"Oh, thank you, thank you," Brother Reese kept repeating over and over as he grabbed my hand and pumped it up and down like the handle to our outside well.

Now, I'm here to tell you, people should not lie—especially at church—because it always gets you in a lot of trouble. The ward Christmas program is something I rank right up there with having the Willey family portrait taken or a root canal. It's something I know I ought to do about once a year but I dread it and avoid it if I can. Don't really know what came over me. Must have been prenatal or postnasal womanopause or something.

"Feel free to be as creative as you want," Brother Reese continued. "This is your baby"—he glanced awkwardly down at my bulging middle—"you know what I mean; you call the shots."

Call the shots? I thought. *He thinks I look like I swallowed a basketball too. Everybody thinks about basketballs when they look at me.*

"No problem, Brother Reese," I lied again. "Are you sure you don't want to call me as nursery leader, Boy Scout winter camp director, or ward choir mistress, or something else while you're at it?"

"Oh, Sister Willey, you're such a kidder," Brother Reese smiled, sucking air through his teeth. "You're sure not the same old stick in the mud. That's why we thought you'd come up with something different. We'd really like it if you could get the less active people in the ward involved if possible; make this a positive fellowshipping tool, if you know what I mean."

You see, Mormons generally take their ward activities very seriously and like them to serve a dual purpose, such as have fun *and* promote Christian charity. That means if you play basketball down at the church rec hall with a bunch of guys from the ward, you're *not* suppose to try to really hurt each other when you foul.

Mormons around these parts call other Mormons "active" if they show up to church at least once or twice a month and "less active" if the only time they're likely to show up at church is in a nice casket. So befriending our brothers and sisters in the gospel, otherwise known as fellowshipping, is a big part of active Mormon life.

"Is that all, Brother Reese?"

"We know this is a lot to ask, Sister Willey, but we couldn't think of anyone else with the skills to pull this off. We thought if we gave you several weeks to work on it, it wouldn't be too much of a burden on you."

Couldn't think of anybody else that would be dumb enough to say yes, I thought.

Well, folks, that's how all this Christmas program business got started. So much for being a clueless, pregnant bishop's wife. Didn't get me any special privileges at all.

Chapter Two

When the bishop, alias six-foot, four-inch Vern, in a gray suit and polished cowboy boots, waltzed into the house after meetings that Sunday evening, I met him at the front door in the throes of a fully feathered panic attack.

"Why did you let them put me in charge of the Christmas program this year! Do you want me to have a nervous breakdown or something?" I clucked like a hen with her neck on the chopping block.

"You'll do fine, LaRue. Don't make such a big deal out of everything," Vern droned.

"Do you want to know how huge I'm going to be by Christmas?" I asked, with my finger aimed squarely at Vern's nose.

"No."

"Do you know how much work it takes to get ready for Christmas when your husband's always gone, you have eight children, and you're so pregnant you can't even waddle to the car, let alone fit behind the steering wheel? What were you thinking, Vern? I can't do this. First you let them ask me to teach in Relief Society. Then you let them ask me to teach in Sunday School. Now the Christmas program. What were you thinking? If you pile one more thing on me I'm going to . . . Vern?"

Vern calmly unpinned his arms from the front door, sauntered past me, slid off his suit jacket, settled into the green velvet re-cliner, and buried his face in the sports sec-tion of the *Deseret News*.

"Vernon Milford Willey, don't you ignore me." I tend to use full names when I'm in the middle of a nicely played out tissy fit.

"Oh, LaRue. Calm down."

Should have had all my nerves crash and burn right then and there in front of Vern—smoke shooting from my ears—gone stark raving daffy, that's what I shoulda done. Would have served him right. But I figured he wouldn't notice anyway, so I fixed dinner instead. It sort of bugs me that whenever I get good and ready to have an honest-to-goodness nervous breakdown, I have to get up and fix supper. But I have learned, after more than two decades of married life with a man who refuses to panic even when I'm having his babies upside down, that I'm destined to play out my dramatic scenes without a sympathetic audience.

Every time I get to the climactic point of a dramatic speech or a bona fide life-and-death situation, Vern yawns, starts reading the newspaper, or falls asleep. Over-reacting or making a big deal out of something is absolutely no fun when you have to do it all by your lonesome. Vern says it takes too much energy to be dramatic. He'd make a downright boring character in a romance novel. He'd start snoring right when things got interesting.

Well, later at the supper table I tried to enlist my children's support after we finished up our Willey family devotional. Vern and I have learned through much trial and error that the easiest way to follow our prophet's counsel and study the scriptures together as a family is to place Book of Mormon or Bible reading sessions *between* dinner and dessert. That way, the kids don't run off when you pick up the holy book and start to read.

After Vern finished reading from the Book of Mormon and the kids dug in on the brownies and ice cream, I asked, "Hey, you guys, what would be your idea of a really superterrific ward Christmas program? food? dancing? Santa? the Nativity on video?"

"Don't make me wear Dad's bathrobe, Mom," thirteen-year-old Aaron piped up. "I've worn Dad's bathrobe and the kitchen towel three years straight."

"Can I be an angel?" Katie, our toothless first grader, interrupted. "I got fairy wings and a sparkle wand."

"Food, definitely, lots and lots of food," Emily, our BYU coed, mumbled, devouring her second frosted brownie.

"Whatever you do, Mom, use John from Maeser House," Amber, our high school junior, added. "He'd love that. You should've seen him at the Special Olympics this summer. He saw his friend fall down during a race, and he ran back and helped his buddy get up before they joined arms and skipped across the finish line together."

Twenty-year-old, two-hundred-pound John from Maeser House has the mind of a two-year-old. He always sits on the front row of the chapel during sacrament meeting next to his caregiver, scribbling large ink circles and squiggly lines in a spiral notebook. People in our ward have grown accustomed to John and his friends from the care facility everybody calls Maeser House.

Their outbursts during our meetings on Sunday don't cause even the batting of an eye anymore. They're just part of our ward family. Kinda like when Beatrice Beebe hollers, I guess. Once you're part of a ward, you're kin. A Mormon ward is the place that, when you go there, they have to let you in. Only visitors, who don't know John and his friends, turn and stare when they make strange noises. I like having the folks from Maeser House in our ward. They tend to knock off your rough edges and make a soft place in your heart.

"How could we use people in the ward who are less active?" I asked the general chaos around my dinner table.

"What's less active?" Katie asked, with ice cream dripping from her gaping mouth.

"That's Mormons who don't come to church," fourteen-year-old Ben answered, like his sister didn't have a brain in her head.

"What's a Mormon?" Katie asked again.

Now, before you think Vern and I have been slacking off in teaching our own kids about which church they belong to, Katie *did* know she belonged to The Church of Jesus Christ of Latter-day Saints. People who aren't members of our church have been calling us Mormons for so long that we sometimes call ourselves that too.

"That's what you're goin' ta be when you're baptized," Alisa stated, like she was so smart. Alisa had recently been baptized on her eighth birthday. It took Vern six tries before he could finally immerse this child, a Willey family record. Alisa's big toe kept floating up. Vern finally had to step on her feet before he baptized her.

"They can be trees," Ben answered. "Trees just have to stand there."

"Just make sure you bring lots of safety pins in case John's pants fall down," Michael added.

Michael, a high school senior, sits next to John during priesthood meeting at church on Sunday because John's caregiver from Maeser House is a girl, and she likes to go to Relief Society. John was getting much too big for his church pants, and the waist button often popped off as he walked down the hall between church meetings.

Somehow the vision of Katie and John in wings with sparkle wands and all our in-actives playing trees made me feel smiley inside. Right then the phone rang.

"Sister Valdez," Ben whispered, his hand covering the mouthpiece as he handed me the phone. "Won't say who she is but I can tell 'cause she's panting."

"No, Sister Valdez, the Three Nephites are not trying to reach you," I answered, trying to squelch my children's laughter in the background. "No, dear, I promise. That flyer you found is just a sales gimmick from Emergency Necessities. I got one too. I promise."

The Three Nephites, in case you were wondering, are three of the twelve Apostles Jesus chose when he appeared over here on the American continent after his resurrection in Israel. These three men asked Jesus if they could stay on earth until he came again. In jest, a few Mormons like to give the Three Nephites credit for all the good things that happen in the world by anonymous benefactors. Sister Valdez's just a tad paranoid.

Every time something semi-mysterious or unusual happens, Sister Valdez thinks the Three Nephites are at the bottom of it. She's also convinced Brother Ruben's mug shot was on T.V.'s *America's Most Wanted*. I told her I'd known Brother Ruben for twenty-seven years and I'd probably be aware of it if he were out robbing banks and killing people on weekends. Didn't convince her.

"You can never trust people," Sister

Valdez insisted. "Lots of them act like they're real nice for years, then something happens and you see their dark side."

Sister Valdez called the FBI and the CIA and me—sixteen times—but nobody believed her. That made her mad. She quit coming to church. Guess that means she's officially less active. Now, if I can just get the local food storage store to quit leaving flyers on her front porch, Sister Valdez might be able to sleep better at night.

"But Sister Bishop, there was hydroglifics on my sidewalk," Sister Valdez said, her voice shaking. "I just know I'm suppose to warn everybody in the ward to get their two-year supply of food. The Three Nephites even left a price list for freeze-dried, vacuum-packed zucchini."

"Now, Sister Valdez, the neighborhood kids are probably just playing games with chalk. I want you to take three deep breaths . . . that's right . . . breathe . . . no . . . not like that . . . you're hyperventilating. Shove your head down between your knees! Sister Valdez! Are you still there?"

After I got home from checking on Sister Valdez, I decided I sure didn't know how to have an ultra-dramatic panic attack after all. Sister Valdez could charge for lessons, that's for sure. Mostly, I figure, Sister Valdez just needs someone to hug her when she gets like that—and the bishop can't handle that assignment without raising some eyebrows—so I do it. I like Sister Valdez. Her imaginary life would make a great spy book.

Later that night, after we both crawled in bed and Vern definitely wanted to go to sleep, I definitely wanted to talk.

"Vern, don't you ever feel guilty about what you do?"

"What?" Vern answered, covering his shoulder with the quilt and settling in for a long winter's night. Vern is expert at one-syllable replies.

"Don't you think you ought to pray on things more so you'd know you should get somebody else to take charge of the Christmas program?" I asked, sitting up in bed with my arms folded across my immense belly.

"Why?"

" 'Cause I don't want to be in charge of it."

"Then why did you say you would?" Vern asked, confused, trying to get comfortable.

" 'Cause I'd feel guilty if I said no."

"So why do you want me to feel guilty too?"

"Vern, you can be so . . ."

I huffed over to my side of the bed, hoping maybe Vern could roll over, put his arm around me, and say, "Don't worry about the Christmas program, dear. We'll get somebody else. I realize you have so much to do these days because I'm hardly ever home to help—and being pregnant too. How thoughtless of me."

I waited for at least two minutes and seventeen seconds, but I didn't hear anything, nothing. Then, rumbling up from deep inside Vern's body and out through his gaping mouth, erupted a sudden snore that measured at least 7.5 on the Richter scale.

"Vern? Vern? How can you sleep at a time like this? How can you just lay there and snore?"

Vern didn't answer. But you have to give the guy some credit. He can snore louder and longer than anybody, *even* old man Barney, *even* when it's stake high council Sunday.

Chapter Three

I kept blaming Vern for getting me into this Christmas program mess. Didn't help. I shoulda known better. Whenever things look rough and I blame Vern, it never does a whiff of good. I hate it when I'm trying to get Vern to take responsibility for my problems and he just sits there with his face hanging out.

After a week-long pity party I decided I might as well get to work; kinda like getting up and fixing dinner when I'd rather have a nervous breakdown. Besides, I had the proper fixings of an idea. It came to me late one night while I was gettin' up to go to the bathroom. Pregnant women do that a lot. When you have to fit all your internals and a baby inside an area roughly as big as a basketball, it tends to make your innards, especially the bladder, feel a bit nervous.

I was too uncomfortable to sleep, so I started rummaging through the Christmas decoration boxes in the coat closet downstairs. Inside the top cardboard box, wrapped in white tissue paper, was the hand-carved olive wood nativity set I bought when I was a college volunteer one summer on an archaeological dig in Israel. That was my last single summer, or summer as a single, depending on your point of view.

While I was running my fingers along the streaked, honey-colored olive wood figure of Mary, I started rememberin' that summer more 'an twenty years ago—the spicy smells of the Arab market in Jerusalem, the heavy, wool-robed, brown-eyed Bedouin of the Negev, the rocky hills and blue-green olive groves. I thought back to a star-filled night when I was sittin' with my knees tucked under my chin on one of the grassy hills surrounding Bethlehem. I was crouched alone in the moonlight watchin' real, live shepherds *without* cowboy hats and beat-up Ford trucks like the Olsens back home. It dawned on me that I was actually watching honest-to-goodness shepherds keeping watch over their flocks by night, just like it said in the Bible.

I walked back upstairs and set the olive wood nativity set on top of our piano and stared at it for a while. Then I walked over and picked up the carving of baby Jesus and held it in the palm of my hand.

"What kind of ward Christmas program do you think we should have?" I asked the tiny carving of the Christ Child out loud. "Frankly, I'm a little tired of the Santa and turkey stuff. Every year those kids drop their loaded plates on my shoes. I hate gravy between my toes. I guess Christmas is really your birthday party, right? So how come we get all the presents and you get zilch? How come we do so much thinking about ourselves and all the forgetting 'bout you?"

I walked over to the coat closet and pulled out the only coat that still fit over my huge belly. It was Vern's parka, the one he uses when he drives the tractor on our back acre. It had a splash of mud up the back. Then I slid the wood carving of baby Jesus into my left pocket and opened the front door with my right hand. The stars were shining so bright, just like that night in Bethlehem. We live about two miles east of town, so the street lights don't break up the blackness. My breath looked like a puff of smoke.

While I touched that carving of baby Jesus in my pocket, I was thinking, *Just once in a lifetime everybody ought to get the chance to go to Israel and see the stars, and the olive trees, and the rolling hills, and the shepherds, and all that stuff. Everybody ought to get a chance to really see what it would have been like on that Christmas night.*

Then it hit me. I knew what I could do for the ward Christmas party. Maybe, just maybe, if you *can't* take Spanish Fork First Ward to Israel, you *can . . .*

I sat in bed a good part of that night munching on green olives and Hostess chocolate cupcakes, thinking, planning, and figuring—since I couldn't sleep anyway. Vern snored next to me. He can sleep through anything. Once, the kids put work boots in Vern's pillowcase and he didn't even notice. Slept like a baby all that night. I reached over and patted him on top of the head a few times.

I finally decided to use Beatrice Beebe's technique. If you assign people to make something, cook something, bring something, or have their kids perform, they usually show up to get a free meal or at least to see what's going on. I just had to figure out a way to ask everybody to do something.

Next day I made a list of every single member of the ward, active or less active, and decided to make a personal phone call or visit to each one in the next few weeks before the program. After I got all the kids off to school, I called Brother Lamb and asked him to build a stable. Brother Lamb teaches wood shop at the high school, so I figured he could build something that wouldn't crash in on Mary and Joseph. He also farms down in Lakeshore in the summer and keeps a few cows, so I figured he could lug a few bales of straw down to the church as well.

"We'll be having the Christmas program in the rec hall, so hold the manure," I said, hoping to get Brother Lamb to smile and say yes.

"Do I have ta come watch?"

"Only if you want to."

Brother Lamb hasn't been out to church for years. He's usually busy cutting a widow's lawn or helping the Scouts with their merit badges.

"Not that I don't like church, mind you," Brother Lamb continued. "Can't sit that long 'cause of my back."

"Don't let that stop you. Sister Hines brought her recliner to church after her back surgery and Bishop took out a bench so she could fit it in the chapel. We could fit another recliner back there easy."

"I'll think on it. When you want the stable done?"

"By December twenty-third, if that's all right with you. I'm trying to re-create Bethlehem right there in the rec hall. Anything you can do to help me take the ward members back in time, I'd sure appreciate."

"I'll work on it."

Brother Lamb is one of those less actives who keeps the ward going even though nobody knows it. My husband sits up on the stand every Sunday, so everybody knows he's doing something. But most people don't even know Brother Lamb. But I know he fixed the chapel air conditioner last summer without pay and kept the Jones boy out on his mission to Australia when his father lost his job. Brother Lamb likes to remain anonymous.

Next I called on Brother and Sister Wilson. Sister Wilson's been real sick for almost two years. Started out with double vision. Pretty soon she started shuffling, then falling—mostly down stairs. Mind wandered too. Broke a hip. Sometimes you'd ask her a question and she'd look right through you. Other times she seemed almost normal. Pretty soon she couldn't bathe, eat, or go to the bathroom without help.

Everybody keeps telling Brother Wilson to put his wife in a rest home and get on with his life, especially since she needs her diapers changed now. Brother Wilson tells everybody he doesn't mind, and that's the end of it.

"Brother Wilson, could you and your wife come to the Christmas program this year?" I asked when Brother Wilson opened their front door, rubbing his eyes to adjust to the bright light outside. "And bring an empty gift-wrapped box?"

Brother Wilson seemed shocked. Then I heard a loud *honk-honk-honkity-honk!* from inside the house.

"That's Myrtle," Brother Wilson said, hiking up his polyester pants and tucking in his shirt as he showed me through the front door. "I'll be just a minute. She can't talk much anymore, so she honks for me with that horn when she needs me. I'll be right back."

I settled into the softest chair in the living room and waited.

"How come you want us to bring an empty present?" Earnest Wilson asked quietly, reentering the room.

"Oh, that will be my surprise," I answered. "You'll have to come and find out."

"Say, why don't you go in and visit with Myrtle?" Brother Wilson asked, pushing his reading glasses up his shiny nose. "She doesn't get much company anymore. Scares people away. Those young priests from the ward bring around the sacrament on fast Sundays, but that's about all the church we get these days."

I walked into the small bedroom that smelled more like a hospital than a home and found Myrtle sitting in her metal wheel-chair by the side of her bed watching an old black-and-white movie on the television.

"Somebody's here to see you," Brother Wilson said, trying to get his wife's attention as she stared unblinking at the television screen. She wouldn't look at him. "Myrtle, dear." He flipped off the television with the remote control.

"Turn that back on," Myrtle ordered, using a few other colorful words.

Brother Wilson blushed and turned to me, shaking his head. "It's the medication. She'd be so embarrassed if she knew what she was saying."

"Take off this blanket!" Sister Wilson barked. "I'm hot. Get me a drink."

Brother Wilson frantically threw the blanket back over his wife's lap so she wouldn't expose her Depends.

"She was such a modest woman before she got sick," Brother Wilson whispered. "She'd be mortified if she knew what she was doing."

"Sister Wilson!" I interrupted, trying to distract her from disrobing herself. "I'd like you and your husband to come to the Christmas program this year. Would that be all right?"

Sister Wilson looked up at me, then grew quiet. Her watery eyes focused on my face, then slowly moved down to my bulging middle. She motioned for me to move closer. As I stepped over next to her, she placed her wrinkled hand on my stomach and patted up and down, up and down.

"I'm going to have a baby in January. Do you like babies?"

Sister Wilson kept her hand on my stomach and looked up into my eyes. After a long, quiet moment, I saw a tear trail down her thin, lined face. I stood there for a long time, until she dropped her hand and turned her head away from me toward the window in a blank stare. I reached out and smoothed her white hair away from her face and kissed her on the cheek before I left the room.

"I can't make any promises," Brother Wilson said as I turned down his hall toward the front door. "But I'll try. For you, Sister Bishop, I'll try."

Next I went to Brother Delbert Mendenhall's house. Brother Mendenhall had recently returned from a stay at the mental health unit at the Utah Valley Hospital because he took too many sleeping pills. When his wife, Ann, answered the door, I gave her a long hug and asked to see her husband. She silently helped me inside their small frame house and guided me to their tidy front room. Ann walked back to the bedroom, then returned, red-faced.

"He won't see anybody," she said. "I'm sorry, Sister Bishop. Delbert hasn't been the same since his eyes went bad. Depressed or something. I don't know what to do anymore."

I stood. "Where is he?" I whispered.

Sister Mendenhall pointed to the back bedroom. I walked down the hall and opened the door. It was dark inside. Delbert was lying in bed in his flannel pajamas, his hair greasy and matted.

"Why, Brother Mendenhall," I said, startling him. "You forgot to open your windows. I'll just open these curtains and let a little light in here." I opened the heavy, dusty drapes and walked closer to him.

"Lot of good that'll do. Why don't you get out of here!" Brother Mendenhall bellowed. "Who do you think you are, marching in here like ya own the place? Told the wife I didn't want to see anybody."

"Well, you can't see me anyway, so just listen. Delbert, I want you and your wife to come to the ward Christmas program this year."

"You must be insane. Why don't you get out of here? Didn't anybody tell you I'm blind?"

"Well, you're not the only person thinks I'm crazy," I answered. "Oh, Delbert, just get off your high horse and come . . . you'll like it, I promise."

"If you weren't the bishop's wife, I'd tell you where to go," Brother Mendenhall barked. "I ain't never goin' back to no church. All you guys are just a buncha hypocrites anyhow."

"Well, just 'cause you tell me where to go doesn't mean I have to go there," I answered. "Look, they don't put signs on hospitals that say 'no sick people allowed,' so why should we put a sign on the church that says 'no sinners allowed'? We're all sinners, Brother Mendenhall. Quit feeling so special and join the club. Program's the night before

Christmas Eve, December twenty-third. Starts at six. Oh, bring an empty, gift-wrapped box."

"Get out of here and leave me alone. I don't want your do-gooder, self-righteous—"

"Delbert, that's enough!" Sister Mendenhall interrupted. "That's enough! She's only trying to help."

I looked him in the eye. "And if you're in those pajamas with greasy hair the next time I come, I'm gonna help Ann give you a bath."

Brother Mendenhall took off his slipper and threw it at me. He missed, but only because I ducked.

"Please don't take offense," Sister Mendenhall apologized as I was leaving. "He's mad at everybody these days. Thanks for coming. But I don't think he'll do what you ask. Thanks for trying, though."

Next I went to Sister Melva Dawn Bell's house. Her husband died three years ago, and her Parkinson's disease seemed to be getting worse. The medication helped some with the trembling, but it wasn't working as well as it did in the past.

When she opened the door, I noticed the tremor in Sister Bell's head and hand had grown much worse.

"Sister Bell," I said after she invited me in, "I need you to come to the Christmas program this year."

"Oh, I couldn't do that, dear. I don't like to get out much these days. Older people pretend not to notice my shaking, but the little children get scared. I don't want to scare the children. I'd love to, but I can't, dear. I used to be in charge of the Christmas program myself years ago. Some people said my programs were the best in town too. But I don't think so, dear. Not now."

"Just think about it," I answered, rubbing the sore spot in my lower back. "That's all I ask."

"You don't have to try to make me feel needed, dear. You know I've been the Relief Society president before. So I know about all that fellowshipping business. I'm perfectly fine. The bishop always brings around a fruit basket this time of year to all the widows. That's enough, dear. And you shouldn't be out in this weather in your condition. What is your husband thinking, putting you and that precious baby under so much stress, especially this time of year? I'll have to speak to that young man. When are you due, dear?"

"End of January, maybe first part of February."

"That's fine, dear. You can go now. Thanks for your visit. I'm sure your children need you at home now."

"Oh, and Sister Bell, I'd like you to bring an empty, gift-wrapped box for the Christmas program."

"Haven't you heard a thing I've said, dear? I simply cannot."

"Sister Bell," I interrupted, "the first few weeks the kids from Maeser House came to church, they got lots of stares. But now they're just part of the ward family. Don't let your shaking stop you. You've never let anything stop you before."

"That's just fine, dear, but I'm not retarded, you know, and I won't have people staring at me like I am. I'm very well educated. I have a master's degree in anthropology, you know."

"You do? I didn't know that. How much do you know about the Middle East during the time of Christ—you know, the foods they ate, the clothes they wore, stuff like that?"

"I don't know much, but I have a computer and I know how to cruise the Internet," Melva answered, with a flash of light in her eyes.

"Great. I'm going to need some information on the customs, food, clothes—everything around the time Jesus was born," I pleaded with her.

"I already told you, you don't have to make me feel needed."

"Melva, my children are on our computer all the time—homework, games, you name it. I never get a turn, and we're not hooked up to the Internet. I really need your help."

"Well, if it weren't for your condition. But just remember, I'm perfectly capable of providing my own instruction and entertainment. I don't need to be needed."

"I understand," I answered. "Just help me out this one time, please. Sometimes I think I'm going to have a nervous breakdown. It runs in my family, you know."

"Dear, oh dear. I didn't know about that. Now, just stay calm. I'll do the research. You just relax, dear. I'll have it ready for you first of next week. That will give me plenty of time to cruise around for everything."

I went to the Bellford house last. Thought Dr. and Mrs. Bellford would be a perfect Mary and Joseph. She was blond, tall, thin, and gorgeous. He was tall, dark, and handsome. Bellfords had the fanciest house in town. Mrs. Bellford was well known in the ward as the only lady in the neighborhood who shopped at Nordstrom instead of Kmart or ShopKo for her clothes. People called them Barbie and Ken because the whole family always looked and dressed like they walked off a magazine cover. They were the perfect family, with ideal lives. I was hoping they could fit a trivial event like the ward Christmas party into their highbrow social plans.

I clomped up the front sidewalk lined with miniature pine trees, then rang the bell. No answer. Rang again. Still no answer. Once when I came to call on Mrs. Bellford, she'd kept me waiting on the front doorsteps for twenty minutes while she fixed her lipstick, combed her hair, and quickly polished the grand piano before she let me in. As I trudged back down the sidewalk I heard crying coming from around the corner of the stately white-brick house.

I clumsily plodded over to see if someone was hurt and found seven-year-old Laura Bellford crouched behind an evergreen shrub. She was dressed in designer jeans, a leather jacket, and riding boots. She had the richest parents in town, her own pony, a life filled with ballet, piano, and French classes, but her eyes were full of tears and she was shaking.

"What's the matter, Laura? You hurt?" I asked, slowly walking toward her.

She was silent for a long time before she whispered, "I'm scared, Sister Bishop."

"Why you scared, honey?" I asked, lacing my arm around her shoulders and turning her red face from the biting canyon wind.

"My Mommy says not to tell."

"Tell what, Laura?"

"Mommy says I have to choose her or Daddy," Laura blurted. "She says Daddy hit her and he's a bad man. She makes him stay in the basement when he comes home from work and I can't talk to him anymore."

"Oh, Laura, honey, I'm so sorry," I answered, pulling Vern's parka around her.

I could feel Laura's tiny body trembling while I held her next to my huge belly. I searched and searched my whole brain for the right words, the right thing to do, but I couldn't figure out how to help her without making things worse. Then I thought back to when I was a little girl, to all the times I'd heard my parents, before their divorce, fighting for hours behind their locked bedroom door. Tears welled up inside me and came out in a gush. So Laura and I just sat there in the bushes together, huddled against the wind, and sobbed and sobbed until we heard a loud yell from inside the house.

"Laura!" Mrs. Bellford yelled from the front door. "Laura Bellford! You come in here this instant, young lady!"

Laura jumped and ran for the front door.

Before she turned the corner of her house, she hurriedly wiped the tears from her cheeks with the arms of her jacket and smoothed her hair. Then she looked back at me and whispered in desperation, "Promise me you won't tell Mama I told. Promise?"

"Promise," I answered reluctantly.

One of the hardest things I've ever done was leave Laura Bellford's house that day. Then, all of a sudden like, it hit me what it must be like for Vern. People with major problems like the Bellfords came into Vern's office every week. He couldn't share their confessions with anyone—not even me. The burden of it all suddenly made me feel kind of soft about Vern.

Funny what you find out about people when you step outside the four walls of the church and say, "Hey," or, "Come to the ward Christmas program." Some of the homes whose doors opened to me while I canvassed the ward had smoke-filled rooms with floors covered with beer cans and half-clothed people with lots of hair. Others opened to frazzled young mothers with screaming babies and toddlers stuck to their bodies while cartoons blared in the background. In our ward we have lots of apartments where people are just starting out and are dirt poor, or they are older folks down on their luck. I felt like I was asking for something when I should have been giving something at every door.

Lots of the people who opened their doors looked at me like I was a half-crazed adult trick-or-treater combing the neighborhood at the wrong time of year. *Just some dumb, blankety-blank, pregnant do-gooder trying to drum up support for some dumb Christmas program,* I could hear them thinking. *And she didn't even bring brownies.*

In the past, I'd just focused on the people who came out to church and thought of them as my ward family. It was kinda an eye-opener to see *everybody* in our ward boundaries, members and nonmembers, active or inactive. Our ward family had over five hundred genuine, one-of-a-kind human beings, a kind of miniature Shakespearean drama of the whole human condition. I figured about a third of our members actually came out to church on Sunday.

Try as I might, I couldn't get Ann and Delbert Mendenhall, Earnest and Myrtle

Wilson, Melva Dawn Bell, and little Laura Bellford off my mind. I felt downright confounded at how little I had to offer that could benefit any of them in any sort of lasting way. Only thing I could think of doing was praying for them—a lot. I'd have to think of somebody else for the parts of Mary and Joseph.

Chapter Four

Took me two solid weeks during school hours, but I knocked on every door in the ward. If I'd worn a white shirt and tie, I could have passed for a Mormon missionary who ate one too many lasagna dinners at Beatrice Beebe's house. If I'd known what I was in for I might have stayed home and planned the same boring turkey dinner and Santa like we'd done in the ward for the past bazillion years.

Each December, all humans residing in Spanish Fork First Ward boundary lines bring their own dishes down to the ward rec hall and stand in a line that never moves because people keep butting in—yes, even at church. The dinner menu has never been altered: turkey, dressing, mashed potatoes with gravy, and green beans. Of course, while attempting to maneuver said plate of goodies to the long tables topped with white butcher paper, most children promptly dump their turkey and gravy on their parents' feet.

After eating your dinner with over three hundred clattery, messy, shouty people crammed in one small room, families stand in another long line with their portion of the clattery, messy, shouty children to see Santa Claus. Most of the children scream when they see said jolly man in red, and won't plug it up until their mom sits on Santa's lap with them. Then the children get a brown paper bag filled with unshelled peanuts and sticky candy canes. In the end, every parent in the ward gets a mammoth headache, greasy gravy stains on their shoes, and an hour-long job of vacuuming up pieces of peanut shells and candy canes.

Generally, several less actives show up for the ward Christmas dinner because there's free food. But you know how the saying goes—if you give a man a fish, he will eat for a day, but if you teach a man to fish, he will sit in a boat drinking root beer all day. I wanted something better, something that would feed more than their bodies. I wanted real soul food this year.

Between Sister Bell's cultural information from the Internet, all the souvenirs I'd brought back from Israel when I was a student, and Brother Lamb's stable construction, things were moving along in the setting department. I had the Primary children learning Hebrew songs from a cassette tape and the Primary children's mothers sewing old towels and sheets into robes. Casting for Mary and Joseph was proving to be a real problem—nobody wanted the job.

Whenever anyone in the ward asked me what we were going to do for the Christmas program this year, I told them, "It's a surprise. Tell your neighbors. You'll have to come to find out." Sure did bug people, but it got their curiosity going.

After several weeks of orchestrating the first annual, never-been-done-before, ward Christmas program, my feet swelled so bad I couldn't find any shoes that would fit me anymore. So I had to wear Vern's sandals with several layers of socks. Now, remember, Vern is well over six feet and two hundred pounds. I'm five foot two, and it's none of your business how much I weigh.

Rumors flew around the ward. So-and-so told who-and-then-some that there wasn't going to be a turkey dinner or Santa at the party—so why come? I was getting discouraged. My trips to see Brother Mendenhall weren't going so well either. The second time I went to see him, he wouldn't talk to me, not a word. Of course that didn't stop me. I said a mouthful, but I think he was tuning me out like Vern does when he's watching a basketball game on television.

The third time I walked into Brother Mendenhall's bedroom he blurted, "What are you doing here again? What the blazes do you want anyway? When I open my eyes after I die, the first thing I'm going to see is the face of Satan."

"Oh, Brother Mendenhall," I answered, trying not to sound shocked. I'd practiced not acting shocked a lot being the mother of eight and a half children. "What ever gave you that idea?"

"I tried to kill myself. That's murder. Don't pretend you don't know."

"Well, so? Obviously you didn't succeed. Looks like you got a second chance."

"Second chance? He made me blind, that's what God did. He's punishing me."

"God doesn't make people blind, Brother Mendenhall. He's not punishing you. You're punishing yourself. Looks like you're blind in more than one way, buddy. Where do you get off saying you're going to see the face of Satan?"

"I've done things, bad things. God knows it and so do I."

"So," I answered, "then repent. Don't you know what Jesus did for you? Haven't you heard? You've been a member all your life and—"

"There are some things a person can't repent of," Brother Mendenhall interrupted.

"Oh yeah? Well, who told you that? Why don't you go talk to Vern. You might find out you're wrong. You won't know unless you ask."

"Why don't you get out of here and leave me alone?" Mr. Mendenhall yelled. "You, with your perfect life, perfect kids, perfect husband."

"My mom killed herself," I answered quietly and deliberately. "Don't tell me I don't know. Killing yourself doesn't solve anything. Try thinkin' about somebody besides yourself for a change. There's only one difference between you and me. I believe Jesus and you don't."

"I believe in Jesus," Brother Mendendhall answered, a little more restrained.

"I didn't say believe *in* Jesus. I said, I believe Jesus. Do you know what he said, what he promised me and you?"

Brother Mendenhall just stared at me for a long time. I decided I'd said just about enough and left before Delbert could throw his slipper at me again. Sometimes I embarrass myself by yapping too much. Vern can just sit there all quiet-like and listen, but I'm always putting in my two cents' worth whether people want it or not, and I think most people, including Delbert, think that what I have to say is worth about that much—two cents. When I left that night I remembered something Vern always says—"If it takes a whole lot of words to say what's on your mind, LaRue, maybe you need to give it some more thought." Why can't I remember that?

Sister Bell kept me up-to-date on the authentic menu she was planning for the Christmas program with E-mail messages sent to my daughter Jennifer's computer at Grant Elementary in Springville. Myrtle Wilson kept honking her horn and patting my stomach when I'd stop by to say hey now and then. Vern arranged for some counseling sessions over at Church Services, next to BYU, for Sister Valdez. Once at church I told Laura Bellford that Melva Dawn Bell was lonely and needed a friend, and asked her if she could visit her now and then in between her lessons. They lived on the same block, and I figured they'd both be good for each other.

Vern could tell I was strung a bit tight when he walked through the door after work on Thursday night, so he fixed macaroni and cheese for the kids before he left for his stake meetings.

Later, before Vern got home, I couldn't stand it any longer. I locked my bedroom door so the kids couldn't hear me, crawled up on my bed, and started moaning. I know moaning is melodramatic, but it helps me cope. My whole body had swelled so bad, I just wanted to explode.

When Vern got home that night, I was sitting up in bed, puffed out like a helium balloon. After he took off his suit and tie, brushed his teeth, and put the garbage out, he crawled in bed next to me, and purred. Even though Vern doesn't say much, he sure knows how to snuggle. He'd get an A-plus if there were a class called Snuggle 101.

"Vern, why did you marry me?"

"For your body."

"*Vern.*"

Vern raised and lowered his eyebrows a few times; I could feel his eyelashes on the back of my neck. Then he snuggled closer. He was about to fall asleep, but I wanted to talk.

"I've got so much air trapped inside me I can't stand it, Vern. There's not enough room in here. With all the pressure, I'm liable to explode. How do those women do it who have more than one baby in there?"

"Maybe you shouldn't eat anymore until after you have the baby."

"Don't you want to know how the Christmas program is going? You know rumor has it that there isn't going to be turkey or Santa, and even the active ward members are going to boycott the whole thing because the new bishop's wife is breaking with tradition."

"Everything will work out," Vern answered, rubbing his thumb in a circular motion on my lower back.

"What if I go into labor and I'm in the hospital on the delivery table when the show is suppose to go on?"

"Don't worry, honey."

"Vern, don't you ever feel just really sad?" I asked, turning toward him so our noses almost bumped. "I've been knocking on every door in the ward and I've found out some things that make my heart ache. People open up when you're sitting in their house without your church clothes on."

"Know what you mean," Vern answered, rubbing my forehead with his thumb, forcing my eyebrows to relax.

"How do you handle everything Vern— like knowing everybody's problems without getting down?"

"I don't handle everything," Vern answered matter-of-factly.

"You can't tell me you have all those people come in your office down at the church who confess major moral sins and share their problems, and that sometimes you don't panic—ya know, sit there and think, 'Oh no, what do I do now? I'm supposed to help these people and I'm just Vern.'"

Vern was quiet for a long time. "Mostly I just listen. Can't solve problems for people. I can guide 'em through repenting, but only if they want the Savior's help. What I can do is love 'em. Sometimes all I can do is cry with them."

"Vern?"

"Yeah?"

"Do you think God cries with us?"

"Yeah, LaRue, I do. Sometimes, when I see what people are going through, I think it makes light to call their heartaches and tragedies gifts or lessons. But I know we can cry till we're down and out, or we can know that our Father in Heaven weeps along with us. That's *my* kind of God, LaRue. He's not the source of our suffering. He's the one who makes sure we never have to suffer alone."

Vern's like that sometimes. Never says much of anything for weeks, even months. Then he comes out with something like that and I feel all warm and liquid down to my toes.

"I married you for your body too," I answered.

Vern was snoring inside of two minutes, but I couldn't get comfortable. I couldn't sit up. I couldn't lie down. My unborn baby was doing the cha-cha on my bladder. I clumped around the house in the dark, and looked out the frosted window toward the snow-covered mountains before I decided to go check on the children.

Jennifer was curled in a ball under six layers of quilts. She was teaching fourth grade at Grant Elementary in Springville as an intern from the elementary education program at Brigham Young University. It seemed like yesterday when she left for kindergarten with a toothless grin, worried she might forget one of her numbers.

Emily, all arms and legs, was spread-eagle next to Jennifer. An archaeology major at Brigham Young University, she'd spent the summer digging up Native American sites in Southern Utah. It seemed like yesterday she was digging in the backyard sandbox, conducting experiments in my kitchen cups, and swinging in the old tire swing Vern made. Someday, expect I'll see her in a National Geographic special all suntanned with a leather hat and hiking boots, parting the jungle canopy and stating, "This is where I discovered the Three Nephites."

Michael was down at the end of the hall. Sleeping on his side, arms wrapped around his pillow. He'd recently replaced his posters of Karl Malone and John Stockton from the Utah Jazz with pictures of Jesus and President Hinckley. He was planning on serving a mission come September, willing to put cars, girls, and college on hold while he left home at his own expense for two years to teach people about Jesus. And the money he'd saved didn't come easy. He'd earned it at minimum wage, bagging groceries down at Maceys. I wasn't so sure I was ready to let him go. It seemed like yesterday he was patting my cheeks and wrapping his pudgy arms around my neck as we rode in the sleigh together while Vern played horse because the tractor wouldn't start.

With moonlight shining on her face, Amber was sleeping peacefully across the hall. She was working down at Hogi Yogi these days and going on dates with boys who almost needed to shave. Amber paints pictures, writes poems, and wears her hair like the sisters in Louisa May Alcott's book *Little Women*. I think she was born a century too late, the way she loves lace and long dresses. Seemed like yesterday I saw her dancing in the front room in my old high school formal and high heels with fresh picked flowers in her hair, lisping, "All I want for Christmas is my two front teeth."

Ben, my gentle giant, was sleeping on his back, snoring just like Vern. He has a paper route and an Eagle rank in Scouting already. He often stopped by the Ford dealership downtown for their brochures on trucks. It seemed like yesterday he was holding Matchbox cars in both hands and sucking on a pacifier in the rocking chair.

Aaron, my smiley redhead, was making smacking sounds with his lips in his sleep. His freckle-covered face was hard to pass up without a kiss. Aaron would rather fish than play Nintendo 64. He rides his bike to rivers and lakes miles from our house, and catches fish whenever he can. But he always puts them back because he can't bear to kill them. I remembered when he was afraid to take a bath, and wouldn't let Grandma kiss him because there was spit on it.

Quiet, gentle Alisa was sucking her thumb as I watched her sleeping upstairs. I remembered seeing her on the ultrasound monitor before she was born. We lost the baby before her and were anxious about her health. The doctor spread that jelly stuff all over my bare belly, then—voila! there she was all naked and cute curled inside me, sucking her thumb.

Katie, my six-year-old cherub, was turned upside down and backward on top of her blankets. I turned her head toward the pillow and tucked the blankets under her chin. She was still wearing the bright pink tutu her Aunt Dana sent her last week. Every morning she woke up, ran into my room, and smiled, "This is my lucky day!" I remembered rushing to the hospital in a snowstorm the night she was born.

Then I quietly slipped back into my bedroom and watched Vern snoring in our bed. I noticed the slope of his forehead, the red marks from his glasses, the tiny mole on his left earlobe. It seemed like yesterday I saw that same face, all shining and smiling, across the altar in the Salt Lake Temple promising me, and God, to live the way he ought to. One thing about Vern, he always keeps his promises. I felt my unborn baby move inside me. With my curved palm I stroked the place where I knew he was growing.

"This is the good stuff," I whispered in the darkness.

Sometimes it's the little things, like sneaking around your own dark, quiet house in the middle of the night, seeing all your family's faces peaceful-like in the moonlight, that makes everything worth it. I had somebody tell me once they'd spent the first half of their life trying to get all those people to quit bugging 'em and leave 'em alone so they could accomplish something significant. Then they'd spent the last half of their life trying to get those very same people to come back and visit once in a blue moon. Think I'd rather appreciate what I got while I got it.

Pulling, yanking, and pushing together the finishing touches on the Christmas program—now, that worked out to secure me a place in the right honorable historical book of Spanish Fork First Ward, if anybody ever gets around to writing one, that is.

Chapter Five

It's when I'm not really thinking that I always get my best—or worst—ideas, depending on your point of view. Take Monday night, after family night, for example. I was driving down Fourth North in Spanish Fork on my way to Storehouse Market to pick up some milk—my mind on static hold—when I noticed this brilliant light in the night sky. It had four long beams shooting up into space that rotated in a circular motion and then came back together in one huge shaft of brightness.

I wonder what that light is coming from, I thought as I drove closer to take a look.

Half of Spanish Fork had the same idea. The parking lot in front of the new Spanish 8 theater was packed. The huge promotional spotlight in front of the new movie house was attracting people like flies to a picnic. That's when I had a brilliant idea. If that spotlight could get half the town out to see the new movie house, just think how many less active members it might get out to our ward Christmas party.

"Hey!" I yelled out my van window to the kid taking tickets, "where'd you get that spotlight?"

"My dad's rentin' it from some place over in Provo."

The next day I had a doctor's appointment in Provo, about a twenty-minute drive north, so I figured I could put a deposit down and reserve that huge spotlight while I was in town. After I got the kids off to school I waddled out the front door, ready to wedge myself into the van and drive over. But the van wasn't there. Things like this happen to me quite often, so I didn't *really* panic, but I was confused for a while.

"Van? Where's the van?" I said out loud. "Did I leave it somewhere?" Then I thought to myself: *I've got to figure this out. Vern always uses his company car. He never uses the van. He'll say I left it somewhere and forgot, like the time I left it down at the church and rode home with someone else and called the police the next morning to report a stolen van when the car was really sitting down in the church parking lot right where I left it.*

I waddled back inside the house and

checked the clock. I figured I could sit there all morning, or I could call Vern and blame it on a stranger.

"Vern?" I said, after I dialed his office number. "Someone stole the van."

"Oh, I forgot to tell you, I let Sister Kelly borrow the van. Her car died on the freeway early this morning and she needed a way to get to work. I told her she could use our van until I get her car towed over to Parley's and get it fixed for her."

"How am I supposed to get to my doctor's appointment and pick up everything I need for the Christmas program?" I huffed.

"You could take the bus." Vern answered matter-of-factly.

"Vern?"

"Yeah?"

"I don't have any quarters," I said as snippily as possible.

"Ask the bus driver for change."

"Vern, this is not funny."

"Look, I'm sorry, honey, but I've got a customer with me right now, or I'd run you to Provo."

Silence. More silence.

"LaRue?"

"Yeah."

"Think of it as an adventure."

"Vern."

"Yeah?"

"I'm pregnant, Vern," I said, my voice rising in pitch and velocity. "Remember? Hello? I might need a way to get to the hospital or something!"

"LaRue, don't make such a big deal out of everything. You'll be fine."

"Vern?"

"Yeah?"

"Don't talk to me."

I can't believe I said that. I've been trying to get this man to talk to me for twenty-five years and I said, "Don't talk to me?"

I rummaged through my purse and found a dollar, then slogged out to the end of the road, and waited for the bus. The UTA bus comes every hour at the end of our street. Of course, there is not a bench to wait on out in the county between Spanish Fork and Mapleton, so I stood in the cold next to three frosted tumbleweeds, my stomach protruding into the icy canyon wind, and waited until my teeth were chattering and my nose went blue.

When the bus finally pulled up I had a hard time making my legs move, and I had to go to the bathroom so bad I was afraid of what might happen.

"I don't have any quarters. Do you have change for a dollar?" I finally managed to chatter to the bus driver.

"Look, lady," the bus driver answered, looking me over. "You think you're special or something? It says right here in stainless steel, you gotta have quarters."

I tromped up the bus steps, took the dollar bill, rolled it up, and stuffed it into the coin slot hole.

"Don't talk to me," I said, glaring at the driver.

The bus driver did a quick double take, closed the door, and waited for me to find a seat. My whole body ached. I reached around and rubbed my back, and let out a long, slow moan.

"What's the matter, lady, you having your baby or something?" a little boy in the seat in front of me asked. His mother told him to hush up and made him turn around and sit back down.

Forty-five minutes and seventeen bus stops later, I dragged myself into the doctor's office and headed for the nearest bathroom before I checked in. Then I sat down in a chair in the waiting room. I was definitely in a very disagreeable mood. After they called my name, I followed a nurse down the hall into the intimidation chamber with the scales.

"Now, just step up here and I'll take your weight, dear," the skinny young nurse smiled, while she flipped her bouncy hair and tapped her chart with a pen that was as skinny as she was.

"No," I answered. "I know I'm gaining weight and I don't need you to rub it in."

"Mrs. Willey. I have to get your weight. Doctor's orders."

"No."

That must be why Vern relies on one-word communication. Some words pretty much cover everything you want to say, real short-like.

"Well," the nurse huffed. "I'll just have to speak to the doctor about this!"

I sat on a chair in the hall and waited. It had taken me nine pregnancies, one too many Christmas programs, and a very long bus ride, but I'd finally made one small step for pregnant women everywhere—one giant leap for LaRue Willey.

I heard a lot of whispering behind closed doors, and several nurses peeked at me from examination room number 2. I waved at them. When I was finally ushered into a room and the doctor walked in, I just stared at him.

"Now, LaRue, what's this I hear about you giving my nurses a hard time? You know I have to chart your weight gain."

"Tough."

"Now, be a good girl and get up on those scales."

"No."

"All right. How about measuring you? Can I do that? And how about an ultrasound test to see what position this little . . . girl or boy?"

"Boy."

"Boy is it? LaRue? You all right?"

The doctor spread some cold jelly on my bare tummy, then ran an instrument back and forth slowly while he looked at a monitor on the other side of the examination table.

"No. I'm not all right," I answered in a gush. "I'm tired of being fat and miserable. I'm tired of being swollen and never getting any sleep at night. I'm tired of this back ache. I'm tired of Braxton Hick-ing every five minutes. My husband's gone all the time, and I'm in charge of the Christmas program, and nobody's going to show up because there's no free turkey, and Vern let Mrs. Kelly take my van and I had to ride the bus, and I didn't have any quarters and—"

"Now, LaRue, don't be so emotional. It

sounds to me like you need a little break. Tell your bishop your doctor ordered bed rest."

"I can't. Vern's the bishop."

"Then he'll understand."

"No he won't. He's the one who got me into this mess."

"The baby?"

"Yes, well, no, I mean the Christmas program."

"Christmas program? Surely you're not trying to . . . Look, LaRue, I don't want to scare you or anything, but your baby's turned breech. If your water breaks, the cord might slip down first because the baby's head is not there to plug the hole, and then we have a major emergency on our hands. The minute something happens, call me and get over to the hospital as soon as you can. If the cord comes first you need to get on your hands and knees and put your head down and . . ."

I blanked out for the rest of his lecture. This is not what I wanted to hear. I started blubbering uncontrollably. I hate it when I do that. I look real pathetic when I bawl and I'm already bloated 'cause I'm pregnant. I asked for a piece of tissue and blew my nose.

"LaRue, your hormones are playing games with you. Trust me. This will all be over in about six more weeks."

"One week."

"You're not due until the end of January, dear."

"No, the Christmas program," I blubbered. "It's one week away, on the night before Christmas Eve, and I still don't have a Mary and Joseph. Everybody I ask keeps backing out on me and I don't have much time."

"Now, calm down and take deep breaths," my doctor said, patting my head. "Look, my daughter's spending Christmas with her husband's family and, what the heck, if it will make you feel better, I'll bring the wife and we'll be Mary and Joseph for you. There aren't any speaking parts, are there?"

"No," I answered, trying to act a little more in control. "You just have to kneel there in the stable with a baby and look spiritual. I'll supply the doll and the costumes, everything. Just nod when people come in to see you."

Doc Dillard's my second cousin on my father's side, so he probably thought of me as part family, or he'd never have agreed to this sort of thing. He started scribbling something on a small pad of paper. I wondered if it was a prescription for prenatal lunatics.

"I'm going to have our rec hall transformed into Bethlehem," I kept gushing, "and let people come in, one family at a time, to see the holy family, so they can get a feeling for what it really would have been like if they had been there that night. I'm going to have authentic food, and the Primary kids singing songs in Hebrew, and the Olsens said I can use their sheep and the Sumsions said I could use their goats."

"LaRue. Sounds like you bit off more than you can chew. I'll be glad to help."

"Really? You'd do that for me?" I took a deep breath and blew my nose again.

"My pleasure."

"I'll need you there by five on December twenty-third to get in costume. It's the old yellow church on Fourth North and Fourth East in Spanish Fork."

The doctor wiped the jelly off my belly with a tissue, and I sat up.

"We'll be there."

"By the way, do you have four quarters for a dollar?" I asked.

While I was riding the bus home I got to thinking. Having my doctor volunteer to be

Joseph, and even bring along his wife for Mary, filled in my last gap for the Christmas program. Maybe I could relax now. I didn't even feel so ticked at Vern for thinking about Sister Kelly before thinking about me.

I thought, *What if nobody ever thinks about Sister Kelly because they have to take care of their own first? Somebody sometime has to think about somebody besides themselves first or how else will people know God loves them?*

It says in the Good Book that the very hairs of our heads are numbered. Sister Kelly has a mother, but she's dead, and she doesn't know who her dad is. Her ex-husband's already married to another lady with kids. Somebody's got to think about the hairs on Sister Kelly's head, don't they?

Chapter Six

On the day of the Christmas program I woke up swollen, crabby, and having Braxton Hicks contractions about every ten minutes. In case you don't know, Braxton Hicks contractions are more generally known as false labor. Some guy named Braxton Hicks was the first man to identify the uterine tightening that makes women miserable but doesn't actually bring the baby. So they named these contractions after him. Can you believe that? The man never had a Braxton Hick in his life, and he gets them named after him?

No self-respecting female would name that experience "false labor." There is nothing false about it. You're sitting or standing about anywhere, minding your own business, and suddenly your uterus becomes so hard you can launch fireworks off your abdomen. With all that tightening, your bladder screams, your back aches, and your heart races. This is not false. This is real. The more babies you have, and the older you get, the more Hicks you get. The doctor said my uterus was so worn out, just the *thought* of being pregnant made it start Hick-ing.

About ten o'clock that morning the snow started falling, soft, white, heavy flakes that stay on the ground and stack up. With all my planning I forgot about the possibility of it snowing during the Christmas program. It hardly ever snows in Israel, and when it does it melts before you know it 'cause it stays warm there most the year round. Spanish Fork, on the other hand, gets snow and lots of it in December. I don't know why I didn't remember that. Transforming our church grounds into the rolling hills of Bethlehem and our ward rec hall into a lowly stable quickly proved to be more complicated in the middle of a bona fide Rocky Mountain blizzard.

Wind from the canyon had blown snowdrifts across the highway, making the frozen fields around my home seem like a moving sea of white glass. Cars and trucks were slipping into ditches and crashing into each other all over the place as I inched my way into town in the family van and pulled into the church parking lot about noon. The whole town was quickly being buried in a blanket of white.

Please hold up a bit on the white stuff until after the program, I silently prayed.

I very carefully unwedged myself from behind the steering wheel and dragged a cardboard box full of Emily's ceramic pottery into the church. After I lugged that huge box through the foyer, I stepped into the rec hall. Brother Lamb had already been there and left. A finely crafted wooden-frame stable was huddled in the far corner of the hall, enclosing a manger filled with hay. Huge papier-mâché hand-painted gray boulders and blue-green sagebrush with their roots in brown garbage bags lined the walls. Enormous black sheets of plastic were rippling on the ceiling with small white lights poking through, resembling stars in a night sky.

Brother Lamb had neatly stacked bales of hay all around the room. You couldn't see the basketball hoops or anything. On the stage was a colossal butcher-paper tapestry of hand-painted Middle East inns and shops and rolling hills in the distance. Brother Lamb was like that. Ask him to build a stable and he does this. He's like a disappearing fairy godfather in bib overalls. Later, one of the kids said they saw him out in the parking lot scraping away snow, but by the time I got there to thank him, he'd done the job and left.

I spent most of the afternoon getting things ready at the church before I drove home and quickly piled every member of the Vern and LaRue Willey family troop into the van to enlist their help for the rest of the night down at the church. Vern didn't get off work till five, and he said he'd meet us there.

Around four o'clock Sister Bell called on the phone in Vern's bishop's office and said someone would need to pick up the food at her house because she didn't dare get out on the roads in the middle of a storm. She had enough dried apricots, dates, figs, olives, nuts, meat, grape juice, oil, and round, flat, unleavened bread for three hundred people stacked in boxes on her front porch. I sent Michael. He got high-centered on a snowdrift in the parking lot.

Jennifer was setting up risers in the foyer for the Primary children and jammed two fingers. They swelled up and turned purple. Emily, in charge of creating an authentic eating area using the hand-thrown pottery she'd made in her ceramics class last semester, complained that she was coming down with the flu. She was supposed to serve ward members authentic food while they waited in line for their chance to see baby Jesus and present him with their gifts. The Primary children would provide the musical back-drop to set the mood.

I put Amber in charge of costuming and looking after John when his caregivers from Maeser House dropped him off along with three of his friends ready for their nonverbal parts as the three Wise Men. After they got their costumes on, John's three friends were supposed to follow a homemade glitter star glued to a yardstick hitched to the back of one of Sumsions' goats while Aaron led the star-studded animal around the parking lot on the end of a rope.

"Welcome to Bethlehem," John was scripted to say, bowing in the foyer of the church as ward members entered. "Unto you is born this day a Savior who is Christ the Lord." John couldn't memorize lines, but he could repeat them back if Amber whispered in his ear to prompt him.

Alisa taped a hand-painted sign on the rec hall doors that read, "When you enter here, present gifts that you cannot see to the Christ child. Fill your empty gift boxes with offerings from your heart."

Ben and Aaron were in charge of Olsens' sheep and Sumsions' goats. The Olsens brought down their sheep in a huge, manure-covered metal truck that drove into the ditch and got stuck. When I looked out the glass door in the foyer, a dozen sheep were running around the snow-covered front lawn of the church, with Ben and Aaron waving their arms and yelling close behind. Things got so bad after Sumsions dropped off their goats that I couldn't bring myself to look. It was almost time to start, and the guy from the spotlight rental store hadn't shown up yet and Joseph and Mary were late.

Thirty elementary-school-age children from the ward, dressed in old sheets and towels, were running up and down the church halls and pushing each other into the wrong-gender bathroom. And to top it all off, the Primary chorister called and said her own children had suddenly come down with chicken pox and she wouldn't be there to lead the music.

I put a towel over Jennifer's head, stuck it in place with Michael's belt, and pleaded, "Jennifer, round up those kids, get them on these risers, and start singing."

I threw her a tape player with the recorded instrumental music. Jennifer, still smarting with sore fingers, was in her element. She got that "I am the teacher—I am in charge" look in her eyes, and I knew she'd soon have things purring as smoothly as she did in her fourth grade classroom.

By the time Vern showed up, I was crawling across the carpeted floor in the foyer picking up a bowl of dates Katie had knocked over.

"LaRue, what's going on?" Vern asked as he shook the snow from his shoes and hurried toward me. "Let someone else do that."

"Vern, I don't know what to do. Everything's going wrong."

"There's a guy in the parking lot," Vern interrupted, brushing snow from his hair while his wire glasses fogged up. "Says he's suppose to set up a spotlight for us and he wants an extension cord. I told him he has the wrong place."

"Oh, Vern. You didn't!"

"LaRue? You ordered a spotlight?"

I nodded my head. Vern dashed for the door. When he trudged back inside the church, he went straight for the custodian's closet, pulled out a huge yellow extension cord, and dashed back outside. The next thing I knew I could hear Vern crawling on his hands and knees next to me on the floor.

"LaRue. I'll pick up the dates. You better sit down, honey. Why are there sheep and goats running around in the snow outside?"

"They're suppose to make the church lawn look like the rolling hills of Bethlehem. Vern, you have to be Joseph. Quick, put this on."

I handed Vern a woolen robe and a head covering with cords while I slipped the Mary costume around me as best I could.

"They're just going to have to imagine a very bloated Mary," I stuttered.

"Mom, someone's coming already!" Amber shouted from the front door of the church, getting ready to prompt John with his lines.

"Quick, Vern, in here," I said, pulling him into the rec hall. "Jennifer, get those kids singing!"

When we walked through the double wooden doors to the rec hall, I plugged in the Christmas tree lights that Brother Lamb had poked through the black plastic hanging from the ceiling.

"Over here, Vern," I whispered.

Vern dutifully followed me over to the stable. Several small outdoor spotlights were strategically taped along the floor in the hall, right up to the stable, and highlighting the manger. Brother Lamb must also be a lighting specialist. I grabbed Katie's flannel-wrapped baby doll from the manger, and knelt next to Vern on the floor, trying to look as skinny and saintly as possible before the first ward member stepped inside to see us.

"Vern?" I whispered. "Think I made too big a deal out of this program?"

"Yep. Turkey's easier, LaRue. At least it's dead and it doesn't run around the parking lot. And that spotlight. What in the world gave you that idea?"

"Sorry. I just wanted everybody to have a chance to fly back in time to Bethlehem, just for a minute, and see baby Jesus and have a chance to talk to him."

"I don't know, LaRue honey. Sometimes you set yourself up for a big let-down. You get these big visions of how things ought to be, and then you feel bad when it doesn't work out. Maybe you shouldn't try so hard."

Next thing I knew, Sister Valdez was dashing into the rec hall, yelling, "The Three Nephites are here! I saw them right outside!"

"Those are the Wise Men, Sister Valdez," I answered as calmly as possible. "They're just some kids from Maeser House dressed up. Take a deep breath and calm down, and don't start hyperventilating again. Sister Valdez, stop that!"

When I stood up to go help Sister Valdez shove her head between her legs, I realized something was wrong.

"Vern?" I said, standing very still.

"Yeah?"

"I think my water just broke."

"Are you sure?"

"Yeah."

Chapter Seven

Having babies in real life is not like in the movies. For one thing, the pain is real, and the lump on the pregnant lady is not some fluffy pillow easily removed by pulling up your shirt and tossing. In real life, having a baby is hard, it's scary, and it hurts real bad. But, after all that, there's also real, live, hushed reverence and a wonderment that Hollywood's never figured out.

"LaRue?" Vern asked, sliding his strong arm around my back.

"Yeah?"

"You all right?"

"No," I answered, my teeth chattering.

I stood there grabbing the manger for dear life, desperately trying to remember what Doc Dillard told me to do in case of an emergency. All I could think about was the shut-off valve by the holding tank from our well, where Vern showed me to turn off the water to our house in case of emergency. I couldn't for the life of me remember what Doc said I should do if *I* sprang a major leak in my personal water line.

All of a sudden a hard contraction hit and I yelled. Sister Valdez took one look at me, passed out cold, and hit her head on the floor with a thud. I guess we looked pretty authentic, since Vern and I were still in costume.

"That one hurt," I blurted when the contraction subsided. "Vern, is Sister Valdez all right?"

"Sister Valdez will be fine. Want me to carry you to the car, LaRue?"

"I don't think there's time, Vern. The baby's coming!"

"Lay down and I'll call the ambulance!" Vern gushed, dashing for the phone in the hall.

"Vern, don't leave me!"

The next thing I know I'm lying there in the straw and Vern and Doc Dillard and his wife are staring over me.

"Sorry I'm late, LaRue," Doc said, still dressed in his greens from the hospital, "but I had a delivery at the last minute."

After some quick checking Doc Dillard said, "LaRue, the cord's dropped. We're going to have to deliver this baby right here and fast. Listen to me carefully. I've got some things in my trunk. I'll be right back. Don't panic. Everything will be all right. Don't push."

I couldn't tell if he was trying to reassure me or himself. Then another contraction hit and I knew there was no turning back. This was for real.

"Vern?" I panted after the next contraction ended. "Think I'm making too big a deal out of this Christmas program?"

"Yep," Vern said, stroking my forehead with his broad, sweaty palm while he knelt next to me in the straw, still in his Joseph costume. "The things some people do to get attention." Vern brought his face down to mine and whispered softly, "Hang in there, honey."

Then another contraction hit and I couldn't hold back—I yelled right there in the church like I had a right to or something. Within seconds, Doc Dillard raced back inside the rec hall, slipped on his sterile gloves, threw blue sterile paper all over the place, and started coaching me.

"One nice, long push here," Doc said. "Take a deep breath and hold it as long as you can."

When the next contraction hit, the pain

was so real, so deep, I thought I was dying. There's a moment when every woman who's havin' a baby knows her life is hangin' between two places, and only one of those places is earth. Later, Doc Dillard told me he had to deliver the baby breech and he didn't have time to give me anything for the pain. I felt myself floating upward away from my body toward the ceiling. For a minute, I could see myself, Vern, and the doctor below me while I floated in air that surrounded me like warm bathwater.

"Where's that ambulance?" Doc Dillard snapped at his wife. "Go call and make sure they know how to get here, STAT!"

"LaRue!" I heard Vern yelling, taking my face in his hands. "Doc, something's wrong."

Vern wrapped his legs and arms around me from behind. "LaRue, honey, wake up! LaRue! Do something, Doctor!"

The next thing I remember I heard my baby cry, a long, loud, healthy wail that echoed down the hall and square into my heart. I felt myself swoosh back inside my body so I could be there—to hold him—for the rest of my life.

"He's fine," Doc said to Vern, quickly suctioning our son's nose and tiny mouth with a blue plastic syringe. "He's a little small, but he's breathing on his own and pinking up real nice. A beautiful son. I'd say about five or six weeks early. But LaRue's going to need some help. Where's that ambulance?"

Vern didn't say anything, but he held my face against his cheek and I could feel his whiskers and the tears dripping off his chin.

"You had me worried there for a minute," Vern whispered.

Just then, John from Maeser House, in full costume, burst into the rec hall, lumbered over to the stable, took one look at us, and ran out.

"Baby Jesus *really* got borned!" I heard him yell three times in a row.

The kids told me later that after John saw me and Vern with the new baby, he dashed from the church and ran around the whole ward knocking on every door, yelling, "Baby Jesus *really* got borned! He's down at the church. Hurry!"

Doc wrapped our baby in foil and sterile blankets from his bag, then said it would be best if I nursed the baby to help my uterus contract and slow down the bleeding till the ambulance people got there.

Next thing I know, in steps Delbert Mendenhall holding tight to the arm of his wife, Ann, as our tiny son's wails filled the air.

"Is it real?" Brother Mendenhall spurted. "I can hear a baby. How can it be?"

Sister Mendenhall guided him over, and they both knelt down on the floor in front of us.

"I'm sorry, but you'll have to leave," Doc Dillard started. "This woman has just had a baby—"

"It's all right," I whispered. "He's my friend."

"I'm sorry," I heard Delbert weep loudly between sobs. "I'm so sorry."

I saw Ann Mendenhall clutch her arms around her husband like she was yanking him from a river, gasping for air. They held each other like that for a long time—not even embarrassed if people were lookin.' Quietly and quickly, the hall began filling with people. I saw Laura Bellford, from the children's choir, timidly enter the doorway, holding Sister Bell's shaking hand. Earnest Wilson pushed Myrtle into the hall in her wheelchair.

"Is it real?" Laura asked, wide-eyed, looking up to Sister Bell. "Is it really baby Jesus?"

John's friends from Maeser House came into the hall next, fully decked out in their Wise Men costumes. One boy reached in his pocket and pulled out three marbles and set them down on the floor in front of the baby. Another took off his crown and handed it to Vern.

The last Wise Man knelt and whispered, "Oh, baby Jesus."

Ward members, real quiet-like, kept entering the rec hall, all hushed and sort of choked up. Maybe they felt, just for a moment, they were really there, in that stable so long ago. People told me later that there was a glow in the room that didn't come from the Christmas tree lights poking through the black plastic or the yard lights taped to the wooden floor. For a fleeting moment, lots of people said they heard angels singing. Maybe it was just echoes from children in the foyer, but they said it sounded different, a kind of music you can't hear with your ears.

When the ambulance guys rushed into the hall, I was shaking like the last leaf on our apple tree in the cold canyon wind.

Doc Dillard said, "LaRue, I think you're in shock. We'll get you to the hospital as soon as we can."

Doc's wife parted the hushed crowd in the rec hall by waving her arms and saying, "Shoo!"

The ambulance guys lifted me and baby Christian—that's what we named him—onto a stretcher, covered us in layers of blankets, and carried us through the rec hall and foyer, then out into the freezing night air. Clouds parted; the storm had passed. I remember looking up and seeing the bright stars shining and knowing I'd just been part of a miracle.

Seemed like everybody knew something sacred had just taken place, 'cause all the crazy confusion from a few minutes before suddenly transformed into still quietness. The Primary children stood perfectly motionless as we passed. Even the sheep and the goats outside on the front lawn's crunchy snow had magically settled down.

Between the spotlight, ambulance siren, and John running around the neighborhood banging on doors yelling, people got kind of curious, I guess. They told me later that a line kept forming for several more hours around the church. People right off the street kept coming inside to see the place where it happened, people who hadn't seen the inside of a church for years. Mary, Joseph, and baby Jesus weren't even there and still they came. Me, Vern, baby Christian, and Doc Dillard and his wife were up at the hospital in Provo the whole time.

The kids told me later, when they came to see their new baby brother at the hospital, that people from all over town crowded into the foyer and waited for their turn to enter the church hall. They wanted to hear the story and see where it happened. So I guess things didn't turn out so bad after all, even if I did cause a lot of trouble that night.

Later at the hospital, after Doc put me on the IV, Vern and all the kids surrounded my bed, talking, laughing, and fighting over who got to hold baby Christian first. I looked at all their faces real slow, one by one, and felt a warm-blanket-fresh-from-the-dryer feeling wrap around me.

This sure is the good stuff, I thought.

It dawned on me right then that God could have made it so there was at least one room open in Bethlehem that night. But he didn't. Jesus, the creator of the whole world, didn't have to be born in a stable because there was no room for him in the inn, but he was. I guess life is supposed to have a few mess-ups—and miracles.

I got to thinking, Jesus didn't have to atone for my sins, but he did because he loves me, LaRue Mess-up Willey, and everybody else in the whole wide world, whether we love him back or not. I like knowing that—especially when I regularly make such a case of things.

"Baby Jesus *really* got borned!" just like John yelled while he banged on doors that night. Sometimes, when I start feeling like I'm not much, I remember that—and the reverence and wonderment never leave.